KV-259-919

For my lovely little Felix

A TEMPLAR BOOK

First published in the UK in 2022 by Templar Books,
an imprint of Bonnier Books UK
4th Floor, Victoria House,
Bloomsbury Square, London WC1B 4DA
Owned by Bonnier Books
Sveavägen 56, Stockholm, Sweden
www.bonnierbooks.co.uk

Text and illustration copyright © 2022 by Frann Preston-Gannon
Design copyright © 2022 by Templar Books

1 3 5 7 9 10 8 6 4 2

All rights reserved

ISBN 978-1-78741-925-4

Edited by Alison Ritchie
Designed by Genevieve Webster
Production by Nick Read
Printed in China

FSC
www.fsc.org
MIX
Paper from
responsible sources
FSC® C104723

templar
books

THIS BOOK BELONGS TO:

_____

_____

C017247488

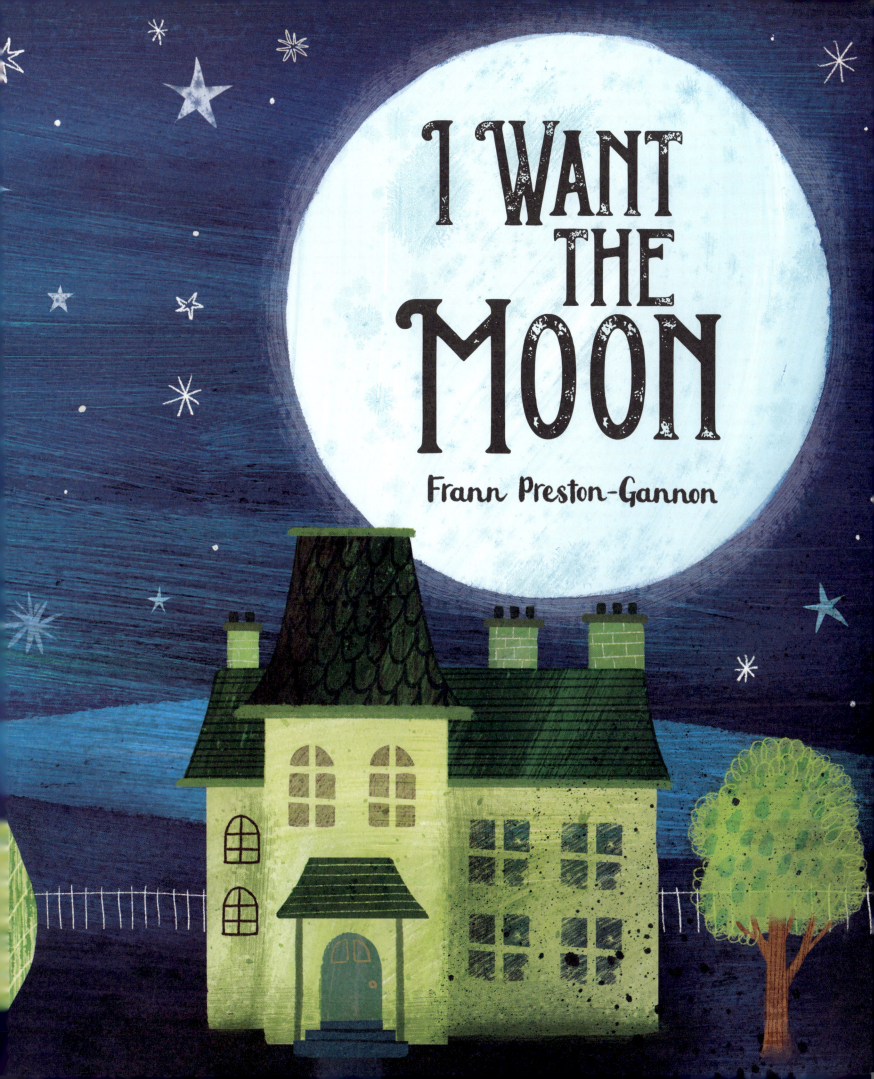

I WANT THE MOON

Frann Preston-Gannon

Once long ago
there was a very small lad,
who lived in a house
with his mum and his dad.

Like most little children, the boy often cried.
His parents were not fond of noise so they tried
ALL that they could to stop the boy's riot,
giving toys, gifts and treats to keep the child quiet.

More and more things . . .
The toys mounted high.
But whatever they did,
he continued to cry.

They gave train sets
and chocolates
and numerous screens.
But the unhappy child
just kept up the screams.

They thought a new friend might help and therefore
they scheduled a play date with the boy from next door.

But things did not go according to plan.
"THAT TOY IS MINE!" Then the fighting began.

They yanked and they wrenched and they pulled and they grabbed.
They snatched and they slapped and they jibbed and they jabbed.
And then . . .

"ENOUGH!" cried the grown-ups. It was time now to go.
Instead of a friend, the boy gained a foe.

One furious night,
his rage reached a peak.
He tore and he broke
and he stamped with his feet.

Clamping their hands
firmly over their ears,
his parents called out
over all of the tears.
"WHATEVER YOU WANT
WE WILL BUY IT!"
they cried.

"I want the moon . . ." the small boy replied.

"We can't give you the moon," they nervously laughed.
"The moon's not for owning, so let's not be daft."

But the boy was distraught and try as they might,
they couldn't subdue him and his howls filled the night.

Many moons later
that small boy was grown.
He was now a tall man
and was very well known.

He was rich and important,
he lived like a king.

He had all that he wanted
except for one thing . . .

Working late at his desk in the office one night,
the man raised his head as the space filled with light.
Moonbeams and memories flooded the room,
as did his longing of owning the moon.

Why not, thought the man. *I'm very rich now.*
There's no one to stop me . . . but I need to think how . . .

So he called a big meeting
with all of his team.
They drew up the plans
for a 'Get Moon' machine.

His factories got running as fast as they could.
His workers worked hard as he knew that they would.

With the parts now all ready, he needed a place
to build his machine. Yes, he needed more space.

He got a big digger and a big metal tool.

He knocked down the homes and he flattened the school.

Some people protested, and their anger grew loud.

The man looked down at the gathering crowd.

Who were these silly small folk anyway?

He wouldn't let anyone get in his way.

With his people all working for the man's great desire,

the 'Get Moon' machine soon got higher and higher.

Until one night came the most welcome news . . .
The man straightened his hat and he did up his shoes.
And with one giant step, he started to rise
faster and faster towards his big prize.

His dreams would come true
after all of this time.
He lifted his hands and then . . .

He couldn't believe it –
the man's childhood foe!
But the moon would be his.
He would never let go.

They yanked and they wrenched and they pulled and they grabbed.
They snatched and they slapped and they jibbed and they jabbed.

And then . . . A terrible thing – the bright glowing ball
slipped from their grasp and began to fall.

The two greedy men and their big selfish clash
tore the moon from the sky and then came the great . . .

The men hung their heads
at this terrible deed;
the shards at their feet,
the result of their greed.

The townsfolk all gathered
in sadness and fright,
to lose their one moon
from the skies of the night.

Then the children cried out,
"We can fix it with glue!"
And the adults joined in
and got busy too.
Side by side,
they worked into the night,
mending and sticking
to make it all right.

As the final piece
was put back in the sphere,
from the whole crowd rose
an almighty cheer.

And working together
to right what was wronged,
the men put the moon back
where it belonged.

Mended but different, it hung in the sky.
Now a warning to all, a reminder why
beautiful things are likely to break
if you take
and you take
and you take
and you take.

More picture books by Frann Preston-Gannon:

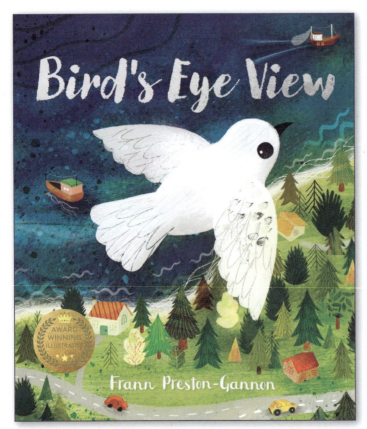

ISBN:978-1-78741-684-0

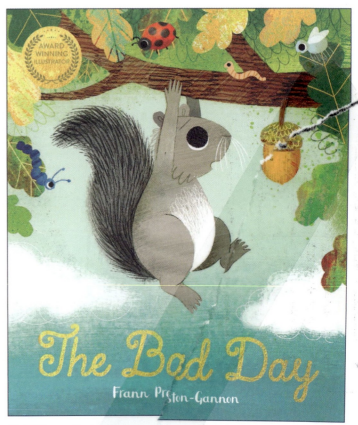

ISBN:978-1-78741-565-2

ISBN: 978-1-78741-385-6